Dear Parents and Teachers,

In an easy-reader format, **My Readers** introduce classic stories to children who are learning to read. Favorite characters and time-tested tales are the basis for **My Readers**, which are available in three levels:

1 **Level One** is for the emergent reader and features repetitive language and word clues in the illustrations.

2 **Level Two** is for more advanced readers who still need support saying and understanding some words. Stories are longer with word clues in the illustrations.

3 **Level Three** is for independent, fluent readers who enjoy working out occasional unfamiliar words. The stories are longer and divided into chapters.

Encourage children to select books based on interests, not reading levels. Read aloud with children, showing them how to use the illustrations for clues. With adult guidance and rereading, children will eventually read the desired book on their own.

Here are some ways you might want to use this book with children:

- Talk about the title and the cover illustrations. Encourage the child to use these to predict what the story is about.
- Discuss the interior illustrations and try to piece together a story based on the pictures. Does the child want to change or adjust his first prediction?
- After children reread a story, suggest they retell or act out a favorite part.

My Readers will not only help children become readers, they will serve as an introduction to some of the finest classic children's books available today.

—LAURA ROBB
Educator and Reading Consultant

For activities and reading tips, visit myreadersonline.com.

An Imprint of Macmillan Children's Publishing Group
THE CAT, THE RAT, AND THE BASEBALL BAT.

Printed in China by Toppan Leefung Printing Ltd., Dongguan City, Guangdong Province.
For information, address Square Fish, 175 Fifth Avenue, New York, NY 10010.

Library of Congress Cataloging-in-Publication Data Available

ISBN 978-1-250-02773-3 (hardcover)
1 3 5 7 9 10 8 6 4 2
ISBN 978-1-250-02774-0 (paperback)
1 3 5 7 9 10 8 6 4 2

Book design by Patrick Collins/Véronique Lefèvre Sweet

Square Fish logo designed by Filomena Tuosto

Previously published in similar form in *The Cat on the Mat Is Flat*
by Feiwel and Friends, an imprint of Macmillan.

First My Readers Edition: 2013

myreadersonline.com
mackids.com

This is a Level 1 book

Lexile 300L

The Cat, the Rat, and the Baseball Bat

Andy Griffiths

Illustrated by
Terry Denton

Macmillan Children's Publishing Group
New York

The cat sat.
The cat sat on the mat.

The cat sat on the mat
and as it sat,
it saw a rat.

The cat jumped up
and chased
the rat

around
and around

and around
the mat.

The rat did not like
being chased by the cat,

and after three laps
around the mat

the rat said,
“That’s enough of that!”

And it went
and got . . .

a baseball bat.

The rat
chased the cat.

The rat
chased the cat
with the
baseball bat

around
and around

and around
the mat
until . . .

KER

SPLAT!

Never again
did that cat
chase the rat—

the cat
was much too flat
for that.